# The Gryffenstrykke

**Written by** John Parsons
**Illustrated by** Dennis Juan Ma

## Contents

**1** Unleashed! **4**

**2** An Icy Rescue **12**

**3** A Glimmer of Hope **22**

**4** Skurdelgrymm Awakes **31**

**5** Never Again **44**

# Meet the Characters

**Ulversen**

One of the villagers from the north of the fjord.

**Sigridsdottir**

One of the villagers from the south of the fjord.

**The gryffenstrykke**

(pronounced "*grifen-strike*")
A terrifying monster.

**Skurdelgrymm**

An evil troll.

**Trygger**

Sigridsdottir's brother.

Dear Reader

How often have we blamed someone else for something they never did? It's easy to grumble about other people, especially if they live somewhere different, or we don't normally have anything to do with them.

But sometimes, as this story shows, making the effort to talk can save a lot of misunderstanding!

John Parsons
Author

## The Fjord

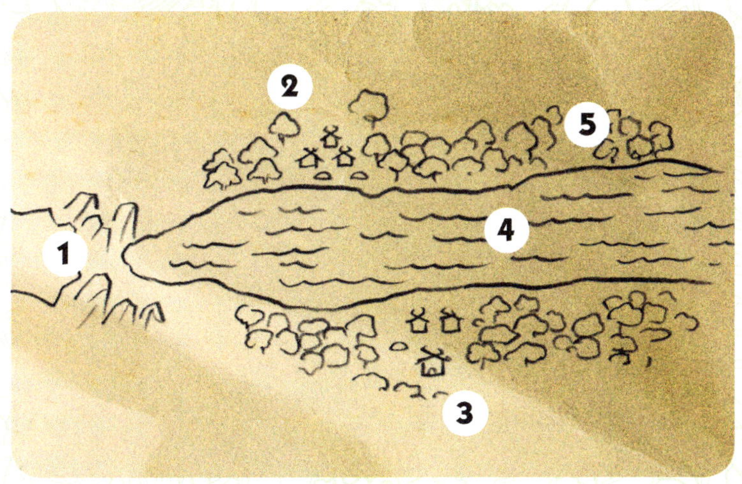


1. Skurdelgrymm's ice cave
2. The Nordsfolkers' village
3. The Southerners' village
4. The fjord
5. Ulversen's clearing

# 1 Unleashed!

The black waters of the icy-cold fjord lapped against the shore with a hiss. Like ancient secrets whispered between souls fixed in stone, a cold breeze seemed to wisp shadows between the rocks. Creeping across the land, an icy mist dampened sounds and spirits.

Behind the heavy doors of the huts on the northern side of the fjord, this was a time of fear and dread.

A lone figure could be seen, hurrying from hut to hut.

Nordsfolk! Beware the breath of Skurdelgrymm. The Southerners have woken the ice troll.

"Nordsfolk! Beware the breath of Skurdelgrymm," warned Ulversen as he reached each hut. "The Southerners have woken the ice troll." He ran to the next hut. "The gryffensmåne is upon us," he whispered, pointing to the yellow moon above the jagged ice at the head of the fjord.

Each warrior came forth bearing a sword or battleaxe. "Ulversen, we are ready," they murmured.

Families mounted sturdy beams across the doors of their huts. They lit their oil lamps. They trembled beneath rough blankets. In every hut, the Nordsfolk cursed the barbarians of the south.

"The Southerners are waking Skurdelgrymm," the Nordsfolk said to each other. "As we speak, they beg him to unleash the gryffenstrykke."

Each Nordsfolker shuddered. Deep within the blue ice, they pictured the spectre of Skurdelgrymm stirring. Once awake, the ice troll would wait for the full moon to reach its apex above the fjord. Then, when the dread among the Nordsfolk was at its peak, the evil ice troll would unleash the feared gryffenstrykke.

All because of the Southerners.

And so it was, in these dark times, month after month. First the mist, the suffocating breath of Skurdelgrymm. Then the moon, an unblinking evil eye. Then ... the gryffenstrykke.

The Nordsfolk waited silently.

The moon reached its highest point. The tentacles of the mist pried beneath doors and windows.

The eerie silence was broken by a mournful howl.

"Prepare yourselves," called Ulversen grimly. He tightened his grip upon his sword. Suddenly, from out of the mist, came a blast of wind. The Nordsfolk barely had time to draw their weapons before the dreaded gryffenstrykke swooped down upon them. Its gleaming talons sliced the air like curved daggers. A bellowing shriek filled the night.

"If any person's blood is not running cold, that shriek will surely fill their heart with ice!" shouted Ulversen, swinging his blade. "Let us fell the beast this night!"

The gryffenstrykke wheeled around. It surged through the air like a lightning bolt. Ulversen was buffeted by a wall of air as it swept its scaly, red wings downwards and turned for the huts. Its burning eyes were fixed upon one of the Nordsfolk; its razor sharp beak was poised for attack.
Grunvald! Take cover!
With certain death a split-second away, the man named Grunvald dived for cover. The gryffenstrykke's beak seared within a hand's breadth of Grunvald's head. The beast let out a furious shriek. It dropped a wing and swung around in the air, talons at the ready.

Ulversen waved his sword to protect Grunvald, who was still on the ground. The gryffenstrykke glared at the warriors. Suddenly, it switched its attention to the huts. Ignoring the Nordsfolk, it flew towards the nearest hut. It landed on the roof with an explosive thump.

The hut's roof was made of soil, held together by a thatch of grasses and tangled cloudberry bushes. It was no match for the gryffenstrykke's beak and talons. The beast quickly set about tearing the roof from the hut.

As the roof and beams were cut to shreds by the creature, the family inside screamed. Someone knocked over the oil lamp. A circle of flames spread.

Ulversen and the other Nordsfolk ran towards the hut. The gryffenstrykke was bathing its powerful body in the light from the fire beneath it.

For a few heart-stopping moments, it raised its scaly, red wings, like a gigantic cormorant drying itself in a sea breeze. Then Ulversen was close enough. He swung his heavy sword in a wide arc. He flung it, blade first, at the gryffenstrykke.

The sword cut a swathe through the misty night air – but at the last second the reflection of the flames glinted on the cold metal. The gryffenstrykke swung its head away and the sword missed its target.

The other warriors unleashed a barrage of swords and battleaxes. But it was too late. The gryffenstrykke soared into the air with a throaty, angry roar. It circled the hut and, with a final swoop, climbed into the night sky.

And then, as suddenly as the attack had begun, it was all over.

"It flies back to Skurdelgrymm, the ice troll. Quick, bring water!" yelled Ulversen. He pushed against the door of the hut. The door collapsed. Ulversen and Grunvald rushed in to drag out the frightened family.

"At least, this night, we have only lost one hut," growled Grunvald. "We have a month to rebuild before the wretched Southerners wake that troll and his beast again."

Ulversen looked up at the moon, drifting behind the heavy clouds filling the sky. He voiced the thoughts of all the villagers.

"A curse upon the ice troll. A curse upon the gryffenstrykke. And a curse upon the Southerners."

# 2 An Icy Rescue

**Ulversen expertly guided his small boat along the forbidding shore of the fjord. After an hour's sailing, he spotted the small clearing among the tall fir trees. He headed for the shore.**

Every few days after the gryffensmåne, the tides in the fjord were full and heavy. Fish from the treacherous seas at the mouth of the fjord were swept in with the tides. Hungry and plentiful, they were an easy catch. Ulversen always came to this clearing to set his nets for a week. Each evening, he would hang his catch to dry upon roughly woven stands of fir saplings, branches and twigs. It was lonely work, but by the week's end, there was food for the whole village.

Ulversen set up camp in the clearing. He drew a pair of flints from his leggings, and unwrapped the sealskin that protected them. Primed with the blubber that rubbed off the sealskin, they sparked easily. Ulversen lit a small, smoky fire, and prepared his nets. Then he loaded up the boat again and headed out into the middle of the deserted fjord.

The water, swelled by the oceans to the west, was choppy and dirty. Branches and debris from the shore floated in the water. But Ulversen knew that the harvest from beneath the waves would be plentiful. He set about his work.

He zigzagged across the fjord, keeping a careful watch for large branches that would foul his nets. A dark, twisted shape caught his eye, and he was about to head away from the obstruction when suddenly he stiffened.

He stared at the branch again. It rolled over and raised a weak, trembling hand. This was no branch. It was a person.
That's no branch! That's a girl in the water!
Ulversen swept his boat around and it cut through the water. The girl was slipping in and out of view. Her long, flaxen hair pooled like a clump of seaweed as she disappeared beneath the surface.

Ulversen knew he had no time to waste. He dived into the freezing waters and swam towards the girl. He crooked an arm around her neck and held her head above water. The girl did not struggle. Her arms sank lifelessly beneath the waves.

With one arm holding the girl's head out of the water, and the other stroking towards the boat, Ulversen struggled to safety. His hand grasped the edge of the boat. With a last effort, he pulled himself over the side. Then he hauled the girl aboard.

Ulversen did not recognise her. Her face was pale, the colour of ice. Her limbs were limp. She was not breathing. Ulversen rolled her onto her side. A stream of filthy water flowed from her mouth. He pushed firmly on her chest, again and again, until suddenly, she coughed.

Ulversen whirled around and steered the boat back to the shore. He might have saved the girl from drowning, but he knew that the icy waters of the fjord had more ways than one to kill a person.

The cold could be deadly. He had to get this girl to the warmth of his fire in the clearing. The boat ground up the shingle beach, and Ulversen dragged the unconscious girl over the edge of the vessel. He swung her slight frame over his shoulder and staggered towards the fire. There, he placed her upon the ground and found a heavy blanket to cover her shivering body. He threw an armful of fir branches on the fire, and it crackled into life.

He sat back and stared at the girl. Now he could do nothing but wait. All the while, he was wondering who she was and where she was from. He knew everyone in the village, of course. But he had never seen this girl before.

Night fell, and still the girl had not moved. Her breathing was laboured and painful. Once or twice, she coughed. Ulversen sat on a log, watching shadows from the flames dancing around the fir trees.

His head grew weary, and he found himself falling asleep. He snapped his head back and shook himself.

"Better check on the girl," he muttered to himself. He stood up and turned towards where the girl lay. Suddenly, he stopped. Two eyes stared at him. The girl was awake.

"Who are you?" said Ulversen.

"I am Sigridsdottir," croaked the girl. "Who are you?"

"I am Ulversen," he replied.

The two stared at each other nervously.

"Why were you in the fjord?" asked Ulversen finally.

"We were fishing," replied Sigridsdottir. "The nets were tangled. And then ..." She frowned. "Then I don't remember. All I can remember is my uncle's shouts, growing softer and softer."

"You should have told the Nordsfolk you were fishing here," said Ulversen gruffly. "We know these waters. We could have shown you the safe spots."

"Nordsfolk?" said Sigridsdottir slowly. She paused. Her eyes sank and her expression darkened. "You are a Nordsfolker?"

"There are no other people here," said Ulversen. A derisive look came over his face. "Unless you count the Southerners. But they dare not come to this side of the fjord."

"This side?" said the girl faintly.

Ulversen and Sigridsdottir looked at each other. Suddenly, it dawned upon Ulversen what the girl had already realised. He reeled backwards.

"You are a Southerner?" he said in disbelief.

"And you are a Nordsfolker," spat the girl, her face twisting into a look of pure hatred.

Ulversen felt for his sword, but he knew he'd left it in the boat when he'd dragged this girl, this loathed enemy, up on the shore.

You should have left the fjord to do your evil work.
It would have saved you crawling to Skurdelgrymm.
What?
Crawling to Skurdelgrymm and begging him to
unleash the gryffenstrykke upon us!

Ulversen stared at the girl. Half drowning in the icy waters of the fjord had clearly affected her brain. What was she babbling about?

Ulversen grunted rudely and turned on the log, his back to Sigridsdottir. He needed time to think. How was he going to rid himself of this terrible Southerner?

He looked angrily over his shoulder at Sigridsdottir. She looked defiantly back.

"Why do you Nordsfolk hate us? Why do you wake Skurdelgrymm and inflict the gryffenstrykke upon us? What have we done to you?"

"You're mad," replied Ulversen. "You are the ones that raise Skurdelgrymm from his slumbers. He is your friend, not ours."

"You lie," said Sigridsdottir. "He is no friend of ours. Why do you not admit the truth?"

"What truth?" said Ulversen. He had never met a Southerner before, but now he knew that all the tales told of them among the Nordsfolk were true.

They were mad. Deceitful. He was sorely tempted to bundle the girl up and throw her back in the fjord.

"That you Nordsfolk awake Skurdelgrymm and unleash the gryffenstrykke upon us," accused Sigridsdottir. "Each month, when the gryffensmåne rises above the glacier."

"We Nordsfolk?" replied Ulversen in disbelief. "The gryffenstrykke attacks our villagers and destroys our houses because of you."

Sigridsdottir stared at Ulversen. Ulversen stared back.

"Not only yours," she said sullenly.

Suddenly Ulversen was stricken with doubt. This girl, Sigridsdottir, seemed convincing. But if it was the truth, what did that mean for the Nordsfolk? And, he shuddered, the Southerners?

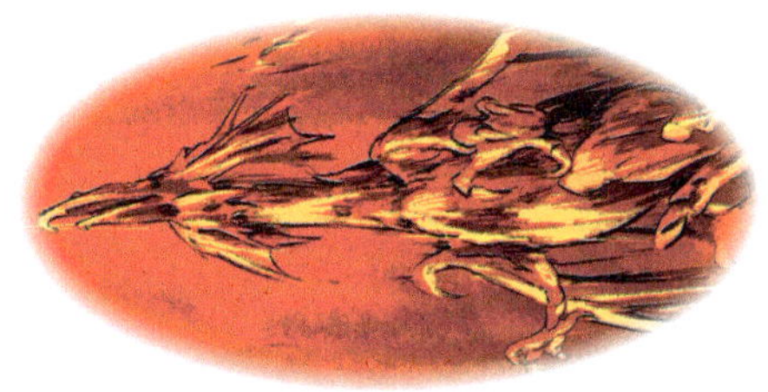

# 3 A Glimmer of Hope

**Throughout the long night, Ulversen and Sigridsdottir compared stories of Skurdelgrymm and the gryffenstrykke. The stories were exactly the same. Only the cause of Skurdelgrymm's awakening differed.**

Gradually, the first rays of the morning sun dispelled the darkness. The Nordsfolker and the Southerner had moved closer over the night. Now they shared the same log, staring at the last embers of the fire.

"If this is so, there is terrible deceit going on," said Ulversen.

"For generation after generation," added Sigridsdottir. She shivered.

Ulversen took off his cloak. He placed it around her shoulders.

"Thank you," she smiled. "And thank you for rescuing me. I don't think I've thanked you for that."

"Southerners," said Ulversen with a wink. "Barbarians with no manners."

"Of course we are," nodded Sigridsdottir.

Ulversen grew serious. "I can't take you back to our village," he said. "They will do what I wanted to do last night. They will throw you in the fjord."

Sigridsdottir nodded grimly. "I know," she said. "Nordsfolk, too, are barbarians, you know."

"I must take you back across the fjord," said Ulversen.

"You must not," disagreed Sigridsdottir. "The moment they see a boat from the north, my villagers will be waiting. They will cut you to pieces with their swords and battleaxes before you even step ashore."

"Then we must cross at night," insisted Ulversen. "I will land you an hour westward of your village."

"What about Skurdelgrymm?" asked Sigridsdottir.

"We must wait three weeks, until the eve of the gryffensmåne," said Ulversen. "Then, if you have not changed your mind, light a fire so that I may see a spire of smoke. I will cross the fjord and meet you at the westward point. From there, we will sail to the glacier. We will find the truth about the ice troll and his gryffenstrykke."

Sigridsdottir looked up at Ulversen's face. She smiled and touched his hand.

"I will not change my mind," she said. "Once in a lifetime is more than enough."

"Ulversen!" called Grunvald from the shore. "You are back early!"

Ulversen hauled in the sail of his boat and coasted to the shore. Grunvald's strong hands grabbed the prow. Together, they pulled the boat up onto the shingle.

"The fishing was poor," replied Ulversen. "There was only one thing worth catching," he said, nodding back at the fjord. "But I'm afraid it slipped away."

Grunvald shrugged. "Sometimes the fish are good. Sometimes they are not."

The two men moored the boat and trudged up the shingle bank to the huts.

For twenty-five days, Ulversen kept his secret. For twenty-five nights, he collected his weapons and sharpened his blades. And, with each night, the time of the gryffensmåne approached. The Nordsfolk grew tense, knowing what was about to happen. Ulversen grew tenser, knowing what he was about to do.

On the eve of the full moon, he kept a nervous watch on the distant shore to the south.

Then, just as he was about to curse himself for being a fool and believing the Southerner, his heart leapt. A tiny smudge of smoke rose through the distance. And, as the spire climbed higher, so did Ulversen's spirits.

My voyage fills me with resolve, he thought to himself. But there was another feeling Ulversen could not shake off. He was nervous about seeing Sigridsdottir again. Her fair face and flaxen hair had been in his thoughts. He was both scared and eager to see the girl again.

Nightfall came. The Nordsfolk called to each other. "Enjoy this last night of peace," they said. "Tomorrow we face the gryffenstrykke."

When the last of the oil lamps was snuffed out, Ulversen made his way to his boat. He pushed the vessel out. Beneath his feet, hidden by sackcloth, were the weapons he would use against Skurdelgrymm and

the gryffenstrykke. Above his head were the stars that guided him to the spot where, one month before, he had returned Sigridsdottir.

His heart thumped with anticipation. But, instead of the usual questions of a warrior – will I see another day? – his questions were of a different nature.

What will I say when I first see her again? he thought. Will she be pleased to see me?

The boat's prow sliced silently through the fjord. Soon, the southern shore was near. He steered the boat towards the agreed spot. When its bottom scraped along the shingles, he leapt out. There was no sign of Sigridsdottir. Where was she?

Suddenly there was a movement in the trees.

"Sigridsdottir!" called Ulversen eagerly. "I am here."

The shadow beckoned to Ulversen. He walked to the trees.

Without warning, a sickening blow to the back of his shoulders knocked Ulversen to the ground. He rolled over onto his back to avoid a fierce kick to his side. He stared up in confusion. With a terrible realisation, he saw that it was not Sigridsdottir who stared furiously back at him. It was a vicious-looking Southerner, pointing a broadsword straight at his heart.

Sigridsdottir! Is this the man?

Sigridsdottir has betrayed me! I've been tricked.

From out of the trees, Sigridsdottir appeared. She stared at Ulversen's pleading eyes and nodded. The Southerner raised his sword-bearing arm. Ulversen closed his eyes, waiting for the final blow. "Sigridsdottir," he said, wanting his last breath to clear his heart. To his surprise, the Southerner took his foot off his chest. Instead of striking a fatal blow, he pulled Ulversen to his feet.

This is my brother, Trygger. He wanted to make sure you were not here to kidnap me. He will help us.

He's coming?

Ulversen tried not to look disappointed. If this were to be his last night on earth, he would rather have spent those hours alone with Sigridsdottir. But he knew Trygger was right. Three warriors, armed to the teeth, were a much better idea.

"Come on then," retorted Ulversen, with a wink at Sigridsdottir. "I have plenty of sacking you can tremble under when we approach the lair of the ice troll."

Sigridsdottir smiled back. "I'm glad to see that you two are getting on so well," she said.

# 4 Skurdelgrymm Awakes

**The glacier at the head of the fjord glowed a mysterious icy blue colour, as if lit from within by some frozen lamp. Ulversen silently sailed ever closer to the lair of the feared ice troll. He negotiated his way through shards of ice that had broken away from the glacier. Finally, they could go no further.**

The blue light from inside the glacier cast eerie shadows over the ice. Trygger and Sigridsdottir clambered onto the ice as Ulversen wedged the boat where an ice face split in two.

"Where to now?" whispered Sigridsdottir.

"This way," replied Ulversen, pointing to a path between the columns of ice.

As the minutes passed, the three figures crawled deeper inside the glacier face. All the while, the blue light grew stronger. Trygger, who was at the front, suddenly stopped and raised his hand.

A massive ice cavern lay before them. In its centre was a strange fire, its flames blue and white. And, stretching its wings, as if coveting the weird light, was the gryffenstrykke.

Suddenly, Trygger lost his footing and let out a slight cry. Instantly, the gryffenstrykke turned its red, scaly head and fixed its eyes upon the intruders. Ulversen's grip on his sword tightened.

But the gryffenstrykke did nothing. Its wings rose and fell gently. Its gaze returned to the strange fire, as if it was entranced by the light.

Suddenly the cave was filled with an angry roar.

"WHO DARES DISTURB MY SLEEP?"

Ulversen, Sigridsdottir and Trygger whirled around in alarm. Silent and unseen, a terrible apparition had appeared to one side of the cavern. It was uglier than anything they'd ever seen. Its breath smelled like rotten meat. Its eyes burned with a smouldering hatred.

"Skurdelgrymm!" breathed Sigridsdottir.

A horrible cackling echoed around the ice cavern.

Are you Nordsfolk or Southerners?
We are both!
Both? After three hundred years, you have finally come together.
That's a pity. Now I will have to feed you to my gryffenstrykke!

If I don't, you will join forces to defeat me. My reign over the fjord will be at an end.
Then why has the gryffenstrykke not attacked us?
Fools! Have you not realised that your fear of each other, fed by the monthly flight of the gryffenstrykke, keeps me in power?

As a moth is drawn to a flame, so too is my gryffenstrykke. When there is light, as you see here, it is serene. But once a month, when my icy breath extinguishes the blue flame, it flies terrified into the night, seeking light. The full moon drives it mad with desire. It will do all it can to bathe itself in the light of a flame.

"The oil lamps!" said Ulversen. "The gryffenstrykke destroys our huts to be near the oil lamps."

"And you frighten it even more, with your swords and battle cries!" laughed the troll. "Fools!"

The Southerners and the Nordsfolker looked at each other. Everything was suddenly crystal clear. To keep his power, the ice troll had turned the fjord's inhabitants against each other – feeding their fear and anger monthly, for three hundred years, with a terrified creature's desperation for light.

"Your time is at an end," said Ulversen.

"We will return with a hundred warriors and destroy you and your lair," said Trygger.

The ice troll shook his head.

No, you will not!

SHRIEK!!!

With an evil look, he began to inhale. Wisps of steam and icy vapour curled into his huge nostrils. The blue flame flickered. The gryffenstrykke became agitated.

"Skurdelgrymm is about to blow out the fire," hissed Sigridsdottir urgently.

Trygger ran towards the ice troll, his sword raised, but it was too late. A mighty gust of foul breath swept across the cavern. The gryffenstrykke screamed in terror as its comforting flame spluttered.

"Trust me!" yelled Ulversen. With a shriek from the gryffenstrykke, the cavern was plunged into darkness. In a panic, the gryffenstrykke took to its wings, battering itself violently against the lightless walls like a trapped bird.

In the blackness, Ulversen felt a surge of air plummeting towards him.

"Get down!" he said, dragging Sigridsdottir to the floor. "It's coming towards us."

The gryffenstrykke, crazed by fear of the darkness, swept overhead. Its giant talons hit the cavern walls and showered Ulversen and Sigridsdottir with shards of ice.

Suddenly, a terrible scream rent the air.

"Trygger!" yelled Sigridsdottir. And then, just as she was about to struggle to her feet and race towards the sound, there was a scraping noise and a small flash of light to her side.

Ulversen struck the two flints he had drawn from his leggings. The blubber on the sealskin wrapping caught alight.

"What are you doing?" demanded Sigridsdottir in alarm.

"Trust me," repeated Ulversen. He laid the spluttering flame on the ice, and hugged Sigridsdottir tightly.

There was a blast of air and a terrible scraping as talons met ice. Then, looming through the darkness, lit only by the tiny flame, came a dreadful sight. The gryffenstrykke had landed. Its fearsome beak and smouldering eyes were within an arm's reach of Sigridsdottir and Ulversen.

"Don't move," said Ulversen. He picked up the flaming sealskin, his hand protected by the leathery underside of the skin. The gryffenstrykke's piercing eyes followed his every move. Ulversen summoned up every last bit of his courage, fighting back the fear instilled in him and his people for three hundred years.

He slowly reached out and, with a trembling hand, touched the gryffenstrykke. The beast's eyes remained transfixed by the tiny flame. Ulversen stroked the gryffenstrykke's scaly head.

"It's just frightened by the dark," he murmured. He slowly placed the flame back on the floor. He tore off his cape, woven from flax and wool. He held one edge to the flame and it, too, caught alight.

The gryffenstrykke sighed and sank to the cavern floor as the flames grew stronger and stronger.

Sigridsdottir strained her eyes to find her brother. An awful sight greeted her.

A figure covered in blood and gore moved towards her. She gasped.

"Don't worry," came a voice. "It's me."

"Trygger!" said Sigridsdottir. "Are you alright?"

"When the gryffenstrykke took flight, I ducked just in time," replied Trygger grimly. "Skurdelgrymm didn't."

Ulversen looked over at Trygger. "Southerners," he said wryly. "You can always count on them to duck, not stand up and fight."

Trygger grinned. "Nordsfolk," he retorted. "They'd rather burn their clothes than wash them." He nodded at the flaming cloak.

"And as for their pets ..." Sigridsdottir patted the contented gryffenstrykke. "Terribly trained."

# 5 Never Again

**A month later, Ulversen and Sigridsdottir sat together in the Nordsfolkers' village. They faced the black waters of the icy-cold fjord. A breeze wisped shadows between the rocks, like old secrets being whispered between souls fixed in stone.**

Behind heavy wooden doors, preparations for the time of the gryffensmåne were in full swing.

A lone figure could be seen, hurrying from hut to hut.

"Nordsfolk!" called Grunvald. "The Southerners will soon be here." He ran to the next hut. "The gryffensmåne is upon us," he said, pointing to the yellow moon rising above the jagged ice at the head of the fjord.

In the centre of the huts, a bonfire blazed.

"Ulversen, we are ready," murmured the villagers, as they gathered around Ulversen and Sigridsdottir.

In the distance, a small flotilla of boats became visible, approaching from the south. Sigridsdottir stood up and smiled. She climbed up onto the log and waved.

Across the waters, Ulversen saw a small figure wave back.

“It’s Trygger,” said Sigridsdottir.

“We’d better get ready,” said Ulversen. Hand in hand, they strolled back to join in the feast that had been prepared to welcome the Southerners.

As they reached the blazing bonfire, they stopped. Ulversen and Sigridsdottir smiled at each other. They both reached out, and gave the gryffenstrykke that

slumbered contentedly by the flames a pat on its head. The gryffenstrykke blinked and opened its beak. But instead of a terrifying shriek, it let out a happy purr.

Never again would the gryffenstrykke be fearful of the dark night. And, free from Skurdelgrymm's deceit, neither would the villagers of the north or the south.

The flames that banished the darkness grew strong in the midst of the village – and in the hearts of the people who lived upon the shores of the fjord.

Both shores.